ONE-ACT PLAYS

from the Edge

by

WALTER WYKES

Black Box Press
Arlington, TX

Library of Congress Control Number: 2008910535

ISBN 978-0-615-26279-6

First Edition

CONTENTS

THE WORKER

The Worker premiered at Missouri Southern State University in Joplin, Missouri, on April 17, 2007, under the direction of Bobby Stackhouse. The cast was as follows:

MAN: Zack Self
WOMAN: Jill Smith
MESSENGER: Caleb Smith

SETTING:
An apartment.

[A nondescript apartment. There is nothing to differentiate this apartment from any other apartment in any other building in any other city. A young WOMAN, also nondescript, sits in a rocking chair, cradling an infant tenderly in her arms. Lost in thought, she is slow to notice the scuffling of feet just outside the apartment door. Suddenly her eyes grow wide— she lunges out of the chair, looks about the room in a panic, stuffs the baby into a bureau drawer, and disappears into the hallway. A few moments later, a young MAN enters carrying an enormous stack of files and papers. He places this stack carefully in the middle of the room—then exits and returns with another stack. Again, he exits, this time returning with a briefcase and a computer. He repeats these steps, stumbling in and out of the apartment, until he has fashioned a gigantic mound in the middle of the room which includes a fax machine, two printers, a garbage can, a paper shredder, several trays of office supplies, a filing cabinet, an entire desk—perhaps even a whole cubicle, complete with wall-dividers, potted plants, and a fish tank. Finally, he closes the door behind him.]

MAN: *[His usual greeting.]* I'm home. *[He loosens his tie and waits for a response, but none is forthcoming. He hesitates.]* I'm ... I'm home. *[Still no response. He scratches his head, puzzled.]* Hello?

WOMAN: *[Offstage.]* In here!

MAN: I said I was—

WOMAN: In the kitchen!

MAN: Aren't you going to—
        [The WOMAN scurries into the room wearing an apron and oven mitts. She kisses her husband dutifully on the cheek and scurries back towards the kitchen.]

MAN: Wait. *[The WOMAN stops.]* What are you doing?

WOMAN: I'm just finishing up dinner.

MAN: It's ... it's not ready? *[Pause.]* I don't understand. It's always ready. When I walk in the door, it's— *[Pause.]* Am I early? *[He checks his watch.]*

WOMAN: No, you're right on time.

MAN: Was there some sort of natural disaster? An earthquake? Is there something you're not telling me? Are you injured?!

WOMAN: No, I just— *[Noticing the gigantic mound of work-related items in the center of her living-room.]* What's all this?

MAN: Oh ... nothing. Just a few things from work.

WOMAN: A few things? Why, it's practically you're whole— *[A sudden realization.]* Oh my god! You've been fired!

MAN: No!

WOMAN: No?

MAN: No, nothing like that.

WOMAN: Oh, thank heavens! *[Pause.]* I don't understand. You haven't been fired ... but your entire office is sitting in the middle of our living room.

MAN: It's not the entire office. Just my cubicle. And ... you know, my desk. And a few other little things.

WOMAN: *[At a loss.]* Do you want me to wash it?

MAN: No, I ... *[Pause.]* All right, look ... I didn't want to tell you, but I've fallen behind.

WOMAN: What do you mean?

MAN: At work. I've fallen behind. I can't keep up.

WOMAN: Why not? You spend practically every waking moment there.

MAN: Well... recently, they've ... ahh ... they've let a few people go.

WOMAN: That's awful! How can they treat people like that? Just lay them off! It's heartless! Don't they have any sense of social responsibility?

MAN: Well, they didn't lay them off exactly ... not in the traditional sense.

WOMAN: What then?

MAN: Let's just say they've been encouraged to move on.

WOMAN: Isn't that the same thing? *[Pause.]*

MAN: I really shouldn't talk about it.

WOMAN: All right.

MAN: Anyway, the point is that every day there are fewer and fewer people doing the same amount of work. They have me running the accounting department entirely by myself!

WOMAN: You've been promoted to management?!

MAN: No, it's just me—there's no one to manage! I do everything! The whole department!

WOMAN: The whole department? By yourself?

MAN: That's not all! I'm also expected to take incoming calls because there's no receptionist, fix the computers because there's no tech department, field customer complaints because there's no customer service! I'm in charge of the mail room, the cafeteria, janitorial services, research and development! Last week, human

resources was let go, the whole department, and I received a memo—
which I'd actually typed myself because there's no secretary—
instructing me to familiarize myself with all applicable state and
federal guidelines! Tomorrow, I'm supposed to start mediating all
employee disputes! I have no idea what I'm doing! I'd ask the legal
department for advice, but I've never studied law so I wouldn't know
what to tell myself! And to top it all off, I have to take the owner's
dog out to poop four times a day! At regular intervals! He has
stomach problems and he's on a very strict schedule!

WOMAN: Well, you'll just have to tell them it's too much.

MAN: I can't.

WOMAN: Why not? Maybe they'll hire some of those poor people
back.

MAN: You don't understand. It's too late for that.

WOMAN: Why is it too late? *[Pause.]*

MAN: Look ... there's really nothing to worry about. I shouldn't have
said anything. I'm just going to have to do some work from home if I
want to catch up, that's all.

WOMAN: Work from home? *[He nods.]* But ... that's our time! If
you work from home, I'll never see you! We'll never have time to—

MAN: I don't really have much choice. *[Pause.]*

WOMAN: All right. Fine. *[Pause.]* I'll just finish dinner.
    *[She goes. The MAN sighs and rubs his eyes. He looks
    around the room, pushes the couch out of the way, and begins
    setting up his cubicle. He takes a pile of papers and looks for
    a place to put them—opens the bureau drawer. His face turns
    dark as he pulls the "baby" from the drawer.]*

MAN: What is this?!

WOMAN: *[Offstage.]* What is what?

MAN: THIS! What is THIS?!!! *[She enters—finds him holding the "baby."]* How many times have I told you?!

WOMAN: You didn't say—

MAN: There will be no children in this house!

WOMAN: It's not—

MAN: No talk of children! No representations of children! No dolls, no drawings, no finger puppets!

WOMAN: But it's only—

MAN: I don't care! Get rid of it! *[He throws the doll at her.]*

WOMAN: What?

MAN: You heard me.

WOMAN: You ... you want me to—

MAN: Destroy it! Burn it! Crush it into little pieces! Leave it in an alley somewhere! I don't care! But it can't stay here! I won't allow it! Not in this house!
> *[She glares at him, then turns and exits with the doll. She returns a moment later with the doll stuffed under her dress. Perhaps she has added a pillow or blanket as well to help disguise the doll. It gives her the appearance of being pregnant. After a few moments, the MAN senses her presence but does not look at her.]*

Please try to understand. I don't mean to be cruel. It's for your own good. I'm only trying to protect you.

WOMAN: Protect me?

MAN: Yes.

WOMAN: From what? *[Pause.]*

MAN: You ... you wouldn't understand.

WOMAN: You don't think I'd make a good mother! That's what this is all about! You don't think I'm prepared! But how would you know? You've never given me the chance!

MAN: No. It's not— *[He notices her belly for the first time.]* What's this?

WOMAN: What does it look like?

MAN: What do you think you're doing? Give it to me.

WOMAN: No!

MAN: Have you lost your mind?

WOMAN: I'm going to keep this baby. I won't let you hurt her. If you touch one hair on her head, I will never forgive you!

MAN: You don't mean that.

WOMAN: Never!

MAN: Listen to me ... it's not a baby.

WOMAN: I don't care! It's mine! She's mine! She's all I have!

MAN: It's just an object. It has no feelings.

WOMAN: She does! She does have feelings! More than you!

MAN: That's enough.

WOMAN: Who do you think I talk to when you leave me all alone in this house?! Who do you think listens to me and keeps me from going completely insane?! Who do you think I share my dreams with?! Not you! You're never here! Who do you think comforts me and holds my finger when you call to say you're going to miss dinner again?! She's more real to me than you ever were!

MAN: I'm not going to argue with you.

WOMAN: Get away from me! *[He grabs her and sticks his hand up her dress.]* Help! Help! Someone— *[She struggles, but he removes the doll.]* Give her back!

MAN: No.
        [He grabs his coat and moves toward the door. She tries to hold him back.]

WOMAN: Where are you going with my baby?! What are you going to do?!

MAN: Let go.

WOMAN: *[Blocking the door.]* No! I won't let you!

MAN: Get out of my way.

WOMAN: Please! Don't do this! Don't—
        [He drags her, screaming, from the door. Realizing that she cannot stop him, she collapses on the floor and begins to sob uncontrollably.]

MAN: When I return, I expect dinner to be waiting.
        [In the midst of her sobbing, she begins to laugh, softly at first, but it grows louder and overpowers the tears.]
What's so funny?

WOMAN: Do you really expect me to cook for you after this?

MAN: Of course.

WOMAN: If I do, it'll only be to poison you and end your miserable life!

MAN: You say that now—you're angry. It's to be expected. But in time you'll forgive me. You may even realize I was right. And if not, well ... I'm capable of feeding myself. I didn't starve before I met you.

WOMAN: There are other things I can withhold.

MAN: What?

WOMAN: Other things I do for you ... in the dark ... secret things ... places I go ... services I perform ... words that I say ... certain indignities that I allow ... what if I were to ... forget? Forget how to do these things? Forget how to find these ... places?

MAN: Are you serious? *[She folds her arms, defiant.]* Fine. You can keep it.

WOMAN: Do you mean it?! Really?!

MAN: On one condition.

WOMAN: *[Taking the doll from him and cradling it gently.]* Anything! Anything!

MAN: No one must ever see it. No one. Not even me. I mustn't know it's here. If I find it, I will destroy it.

WOMAN: But ... *[Pause.]* Shouldn't you ...

MAN: Shouldn't I what?

WOMAN: Shouldn't there be some ... well, some shared responsibilities? I mean, I shouldn't have to raise her alone.

MAN: You want to give me responsibilities?

WOMAN: Yes.

MAN: For the—

WOMAN: The child. Our child.

MAN: Fine. If it misbehaves, I'll punish it.

WOMAN: No. You'd be too harsh.

MAN: What do you want from me?

WOMAN: You could put her to sleep. And if she wakes during the night, you could hold her and pat her back.

MAN: It'd better not wake! I have to work in the morning!

WOMAN: You can't expect a baby to always sleep through the night. And if you're tired, you could take a day off every now and then. You have sick days.

MAN: I never take sick days!

WOMAN: That was before. Work was your only priority. Now there's a child to think of.

MAN: You see! This is how it starts!

WOMAN: How what starts?

MAN: There was a reason I wouldn't allow you to have this child!

WOMAN: Because you're selfish and only think of yourself!

MAN: No, because suddenly you expect me to take sick days and buy diapers and leave early to see it perform in school plays! You'll start calling me during work hours to tell me it's crawling or talking or taking its first poop! Word starts spreading that I'm not committed to my job anymore, and next thing you know, I end up like the others!

WOMAN: What others? The ones who were fired?

MAN: Yes! No! I told you, they weren't fired!

WOMAN: Then what? *[Pause.]* What?

MAN: *[Under his breath—almost a whisper.]* They were killed.

WOMAN: What?

MAN: They were murdered! Executed!

WOMAN: Murdered?

MAN: Yes! Put to death!

WOMAN: Who murdered them?

MAN: The company! Who do you think?

WOMAN: But ... if the company wasn't happy with their performance, why didn't it just let them go? I mean, in the old fashioned sense?

MAN: I don't know. You can't expect me to understand the company's actions. It's a giant corporation. It doesn't think the way we do. Maybe it didn't want them to share trade secrets with the other companies. Maybe it didn't want to pay unemployment. Maybe it just wanted to avoid paperwork.

WOMAN: But ... they can't get away with that! Those poor people! We should call the authorities!

MAN: Shhh! Not so loud! Someone might hear! Besides, the authorities don't want to get involved. And, to be honest, these were not the best employees. I mean, they really did deserve some sort of punishment. Not death, you know, but they weren't pulling their own weight, and it was all handled very nicely. They threw a party beforehand and—

WOMAN: A party?

MAN: Yes.

WOMAN: Before they ... *[She motions slitting her throat. He nods.]* It seems a little strange. To throw a party for someone and then ...

MAN: It was the company's way of thanking them for whatever small contribution they'd made over the years. Each of them had a cake. One candle for every year of service. It was really quite touching. Some of them cried.

WOMAN: But—

MAN: I shouldn't have told you any of this, but I want you to understand my position. They mustn't question my dedication to the company. Not for one moment. *[She nods.]* Good. I'm glad you understand. If I've been harsh with you, it's only because I knew what the consequences of certain actions might be. You can see now that it wasn't out of arrogance or selfishness. I was looking out for us ... for the two of us. For our family. Now, we won't speak of this again. Ever. To anyone. It isn't safe. Agreed? *[Pause.]* Promise me.

WOMAN: I just think ... those poor people ... someone should—

MAN: Promise. *[Pause.]*

WOMAN: All right. I promise.

MAN: Good girl. *[He kisses her.]* We have to look out for ourselves. There's nothing more we can do. It's not realistic. We go about our jobs—do the best we can—and try to be happy. *[There is a knock at the door.]* Who's that?

WOMAN: I don't know.

MAN: Did you invite someone for dinner?

WOMAN: No. *[The MAN looks through the peephole.]* Who is it?

MAN: I don't know. I can't tell.

WOMAN: Let me look.
          [He steps out of the way. She looks through the peephole.]

MAN: Can you see anything?

WOMAN: No. *[There is another knock at the door.]* Should we answer?

MAN: I don't know.

WOMAN: Maybe they'll go away.

MAN: What if it's something important?

WOMAN: Like what?

MAN: I don't know.
          [Pause. Another knock—louder. The MAN opens the door. A MESSENGER stands in the doorway holding a clipboard.]
Hello?

THE MESSENGER: I have a message for employee nine-zero-zero-eight-five-six-one dash B dash H dash three-three-three.

MAN: That's me.

THE MESSENGER: *[Reading from his clipboard.]* The company wishes to inform you that there will be a party held in your honor Monday morning.

MAN: A ... a party?

THE MESSENGER: *[Still reading.]* Cake will be served promptly at 8:00 AM.

MAN: There ... there must be some mistake.

THE MESSENGER: As always, tardiness is frowned upon.

 MAN: But—

THE MESSENGER: What kind of cake would you like?

MAN: You don't understand!

THE MESSENGER: Chocolate, vanilla, or strawberry?

MAN: I'm a model employee!

THE MESSENGER: Chocolate, vanilla, or—

MAN: I've never even taken one sick day! Not one!

THE MESSENGER: Chocolate—

MAN: I'm running more than a dozen departments all by myself! I've just memorized the entire human resources handbook! The entire thing! I can quote it for you! Verbatim! I can quote it backwards! I'm a useful employee! Ask anyone! I'll ... I'll ... I'll work for free! I'll even forfeit my—

THE MESSENGER: CHOCOLATE, VANILLA, or STRAWBERRY?!!! *[Pause.]* Look ... I'm just trying to do my job.

I have to look out for myself, you know. It's nothing personal. *[Pause.]* Chocolate, vanilla, or—

MAN: It doesn't matter.

THE MESSENGER: You have to choose.

MAN: I don't care.

THE MESSENGER: Chocolate then. *[The MESSENGER makes a note on his clipboard.]* How many years of service?

MAN: What?

THE MESSENGER: How many years have you been with the company? The candles. You get one for every—

MAN: I ... I don't remember. It's been—

THE MESSENGER: It's all right. I can check your file. Just sign here.
> *[The MAN signs reluctantly. The MESSENGER exits. Silence.]*

MAN: I don't understand. *[Pause.]* I did everything they asked. Everything. I followed every rule. I never spoke out of turn. I brought donuts once a week. How could they question my ... *[Pause.]* Wait ... you ... you didn't tell anyone—did you?

WOMAN: Tell what?

MAN: About the child! The doll!

WOMAN: No. I ... I don't think so.

MAN: You don't think so?!

WOMAN: I ... I don't—

[A sudden realization. Horrified, she covers her mouth.]

MAN: Who?! Who did you tell?!

WOMAN: The other day, at the grocery store, I ... I ran into that woman, you know, from the company picnic ... the one with no bra ... with the cigarettes and the stringy hair—

MAN: My god! She hates me! How could you—

WOMAN: I only mentioned it to make her jealous!

MAN: You might as well have cut my head off yourself! That woman's had it out for me since day one! She wants my job! She's been watching like a hawk—waiting for me to slip up! She must have told them. *[Pause.]*

WOMAN: What are we going to do?

MAN: Nothing.

WOMAN: But—

MAN: There's nothing we can do. It's over.

WOMAN: Maybe ... maybe you can tell them it was a mistake? Tell them she's lying! She made the whole thing up! Out of jealousy!

MAN: They'd find out the truth.

WOMAN: I'll deny it! I never said anything! She doesn't have any proof! *[Pause. He considers this.]*

MAN: We'd have to destroy all the evidence.

WOMAN: What do you mean? What evidence? *[He looks at the doll. She clings to it protectively.]* No. Please.

MAN: It's the only way.

WOMAN: You don't know what you're asking.

MAN: I know what the … the child means to you. But it's her or me. There's really no choice. *[Pause.]* Is there? *[Pause.]* Surely you wouldn't choose that thing over me. *[Silence.]*

WOMAN: Her … her name is Emma.

MAN: They're going to kill me. *[Pause.]*

WOMAN: She discovered her feet the other day. I wish you could've seen it.

MAN: Do you understand what I'm telling you.

WOMAN: She can make animal sounds too. She can do lion, doggie, monkey, and duck.

MAN: I'm going to die. They're going to chop off my head.

WOMAN: She whacked the cat on the head this morning, and I told her that wasn't nice and she should say she was sorry. So she petted the cat on the head and said, "Sorry, Meow." Then she got the cat brush and started brushing him and said, "There go, Meow." It was so sweet.

MAN: She can't do that. She's an infant.

WOMAN: She's very advanced.

MAN: What am I saying? She's not even an infant—she's a doll!

WOMAN: She can count to ten.

MAN: She cannot!

WOMAN: She can. Sometimes she skips "seven" because it's harder than the others.

MAN: You're making that up!

WOMAN: No.

MAN: All right, then make her do it! C'mon! Right now!

WOMAN: She isn't in the mood.

MAN: Not in the mood!

WOMAN: She's not a trained monkey, you know. *[Pause.]*

MAN: You're … you're really going to let me die? *[Pause.]*

WOMAN: Maybe you've misunderstood. Maybe they're really throwing you a party. Just a party. Maybe they want to thank you for all the extra hours you've put in. *[Pause.]* You should probably get your work done. Just in case. We'll leave you alone now. I'm sure you don't want any distractions. *[Pause.]* Emma and I will keep our fingers crossed for you. *[To the doll.]* Won't we, Emma? *[Pause.]* Tell Daddy, "Bye-bye." *[Pause.]* Bye-bye, Daddy.
      [The WOMAN exits. The MAN remains standing, motionless.]

* * *

THE SPOTTED MAN

The Spotted Man was first produced on December 8, 2007, at the Student Theatre in Malmö, Sweden. The production was co-directed by Dan Malm and Jennifer Howgate. The cast was as follows:

EUGENE: Fraser MacLeod
NURSE/DR. FLIM/DR. FLAM: Maryse Urruty
THE SPECIALIST: Jonathan Alexander

SETTING:
An examining room.

[An examining room—very sterile. Enter EUGENE, a harmless-looking man covered with spots. A NURSE follows behind him.]

NURSE: Have a seat.
[EUGENE sits on a rolling stool. The NURSE stops suddenly and glares at him. Silence. EUGENE begins to fidget.]

EUGENE: I ... I'm sorry, is something—

NURSE: Not there!

EUGENE: What?

NURSE: Not there!

EUGENE: Not ... not here?

NURSE: No!

EUGENE: Where?

NURSE: There!
[She points to the examining table.]

EUGENE: Oh! Right! Sorry!

NURSE: This is the DOCTOR'S stool!

EUGENE: I'm sorry. I ... I didn't realize.
[EUGENE moves to the examining table. The NURSE produces a sterilized rag and a spray bottle. She sanitizes the stool thoroughly.]

NURSE: As if you'd never been inside a doctor's office! As if you didn't know how things work!
[The NURSE continues to glare as she scrubs the stool furiously.]

EUGENE: You're right. I ... I should have known better than to sit on his—

NURSE: Her!

EUGENE: —her stool. I apologize. I ... I don't know what came over me.

NURSE: *[Finishing.]* There.

EUGENE: Listen ... I ... ahh ... I hesitate to ask this, but—

NURSE: What?

EUGENE: Well ... I ... I know this may not be precisely the right moment to ... I mean, I know you're very busy, and this may sound a bit childish, but ... well, I was wondering if it might be possible for my wife to wait in here with me. In the examining room.

NURSE: Your wife?

EUGENE: That's right.

NURSE: In here?

EUGENE: I know! It's ridiculous! A grown man! It's just that ... well ... I'm a little nervous, and she ... well ... she tends to have a calming effect on me. She's like a human sedative! *[Pause—the NURSE glares at him.]* Anyway, she's in the lobby. If you could just send her in, I'd ... I'd really appreciate it. *[Pause—the NURSE glares at him.]* Thank you. *[Pause—the NURSE glares at him.]* She's wearing a green dress with flowers and a little hat that—

NURSE: You'll have to ask the doctor.

EUGENE: What?

NURSE: The doctor! The doctor! You'll have to ask the doctor!

EUGENE: You ... you can't just send her in?

NURSE: No, I'm afraid not. I can give you a little morphine if you like?

EUGENE: Morphine?

NURSE: That's right.

EUGENE: You can give me morphine, but you can't fetch my wife from the lobby?

NURSE: We have our rules. *[She produces a thermometer.]* I'm going to take your temperature now.
> *[EUGENE sticks his tongue out. The NURSE glares at him. EUGENE begins to fidget.]*

EUGENE: What?

NURSE: I'm going to take your temperature.

EUGENE: Right ... *[Again, EUGENE sticks his tongue out. The NURSE throws her hands in the air.]* What? I don't understand.

NURSE: Your pants! Your pants! Drop your pants!

EUGENE: My pants? Why should I—

NURSE: I'm going to take your TEMPERATURE!

EUGENE: My ... OH!!! You know what ... I ... I'd really prefer the other end if you don't mind.

NURSE: Fine. But it's not nearly as precise! *[She inserts the thermometer into his mouth and picks up his chart.]* Now. What's the problem?

EUGENE: *[Astonished.]* What's the problem?

NURSE: That's right. What's the problem? Why are you here? For what reason have you come to us? You did come for a reason—didn't you?

EUGENE: Look at me!
    [She looks at him without much interest.]

NURSE: I'm a medical assistant—not a trained physician. It would be best if you just told me what was wrong.

EUGENE: I've got spots!

NURSE: Spots?

EUGENE: Yes! Spots!

NURSE: *[Writing in his chart.]* And these "spots" ... where are they located?

EUGENE: *[Astonished.]* Where are they located?

NURSE: That's right.

EUGENE: They're everywhere!

NURSE: Everywhere?

EUGENE: Everywhere! My entire body is covered with spots!
    *[The NURSE makes a few more notes on EUGENE's chart.
    The thermometer beeps. She checks it.]*

NURSE: *[Suspicious.]* Hmmm ...

EUGENE: What?

NURSE: *[Evasive.]* Oh ... nothing.

EUGENE: Nothing? What do you mean nothing? What was the "Hmmm …" for?

NURSE: The "Hmmm?"

EUGENE: That's right! The "Hmmm!" You said "Hmmm!" Don't try to deny it!

NURSE: I'm not denying anything.

EUGENE: What was it for?

NURSE: The "Hmmm?"

EUGENE: Yes! "The Hmmm!"

NURSE: Well ... you have to admit it's a bit suspicious.

EUGENE: What's suspicious?

NURSE: You claim to be sick—and yet you have no temperature.

EUGENE: Do I have to have a temperature?

NURSE: Well ... no, you don't have to.

EUGENE: Aren't there plenty of sick people out there with no temperature at all?

NURSE: That's true, but—

EUGENE: But what?

NURSE: Well, it's just that, if you were to show a bit of a temperature, it would make things a lot easier on us. A good fever is always a sure sign that something's wrong. You don't want to make my job any more difficult than it has to be—do you?

EUGENE: No, no, of course not.

NURSE: I didn't think so. Now, why don't we give it another shot? Maybe if we try the other end this time...

EUGENE: What?! No!

NURSE: Why not? What are you trying to hide?

EUGENE: What am I trying to HIDE?! What am I ... I'm not trying to HIDE anything! Look at me! *[EUGENE tears off his shirt.]* Look! My entire body is covered with spots! Spots of every conceivable shape and size! Big spots! Small spots! Short spots! Tall spots! I have a spot the shape of Italy on my back! And another one ... I ... I know it sounds crazy, but ... I'd swear it's the virgin Mary!

NURSE: Where?

EUGENE: On my ... ahh ... on my ...

NURSE: Your what?

EUGENE: I'm not comfortable talking about this with you! I'd like to see the doctor!

NURSE: Are you sure you're not just trying to score some morphine?

EUGENE: No! No, I'm not trying to score some morphine! I didn't even mention morphine! I don't want morphine! The morphine was your idea! I'm a very sick man! There is something horribly, horribly wrong with me, and I've come to you for help! Can't you just help me?! Isn't that why you're here?! To help people who are sick?! *[The NURSE glares at EUGENE for a moment—then makes some notes in his chart.]* What ... ahh ... what are you writing?

NURSE: *[A vengeful tone in her voice.]* Nothing. *[She continues to write.]*

EUGENE: That's an awful long "nothing." *[The NURSE scribbles violently in EUGENE's chart.]* You know, I ... I can't help but feel we've gotten off on the wrong foot somehow. I'd like to apologize if I've offended you in any way or ... or made your job more difficult. That was certainly not my intent. It's just that I ... I'm very concerned about these spots! I'm not normally like this. Normally, I'm very relaxed. Very laid back. Really! Water off the back—all that! You can ask my wife, she'll tell you. But these spots ... they ... they've gotten under my skin! It's almost ... I know this may sound a little crazy ... but it's almost like they're alive! Like they've got a mind of their own! They come and go as they please, pop up in the most inconvenient places, torment me for a while, make little pictures, signs, sometimes they almost seem to spell out words! And then they vanish without a trace! As if they were never there at all! For weeks, my wife didn't believe me! She thought I'd gone insane! Every time I tried to show her, they'd disappear! But as soon as she turned her back, they'd rear their ugly little heads! Twice as many as before! It's like they're toying with me! Little microscopic invaders playing games with my mind!

NURSE: Put this on. The doctor will be with you shortly.
[She hands him a hospital gown.]

EUGENE: Thank you. *[He begins to undress.]* Listen, I ... I don't want you to think I expect special treatment just because of the severity of my condition, but if you could ask the doctor about my wife—

NURSE: What are you doing?!

EUGENE: I ... I'm changing. You said to put this—

NURSE: Wait until I leave the room!

EUGENE: Oh! Right! Sorry! I'm sorry! *[The NURSE exits, hanging EUGENE's chart on the door.]* You've been very helpful! Thank you! Thank you very much!

[EUGENE closes the door. He continues to undress, hiding behind the examining table in case someone should enter unexpectedly. After a moment, he emerges in his hospital gown. DR. FLIM enters. She looks exactly like the NURSE, although her uniform is entirely different.]

DR. FLIM: Hello, I'm Dr. Flim.

EUGENE: Hello— *[Turning to see her.]* Wait a minute ... you're not the doctor!

DR. FLIM: What do you mean? Of course I'm the doctor.

EUGENE: But ... when you were here before—

DR. FLIM: When I was here before? But I've only just stepped into the room.

EUGENE: You took my temperature!

DR. FLIM: No ...

EUGENE: Yes! You wanted to try the other end!

DR. FLIM: Oh! *[She laughs.]* No, that was the nurse—Margo.

EUGENE: Margo?

DR. FLIM: That's right.

EUGENE: Are you twins?

DR. FLIM: Twins? Not at all.

EUGENE: But you look just like her!

DR. FLIM: Oh, don't be ridiculous. We look nothing alike. She's much more attractive. Now, let's get down to business, shall we?

[She reads EUGENE's chart.] Hmmm ... *[She nods, suppresses a laugh.]* Well ... all right. I suppose I should have a look then, shouldn't I? *[EUGENE offers her his arm. DR. FLIM seems confused.]* What's this?

EUGENE: What do you mean?

DR. FLIM: What do you mean what do I mean?

EUGENE: You said you wanted to have a look.

DR. FLIM: Right.

EUGENE: Here it is.

DR. FLIM: This is your arm.

EUGENE: I know.

DR. FLIM: What does your arm have to do with ... oh! I see! Actually, the idea that hand size is corollary—it's a myth, propagated, I should think, by men with large hands. Perhaps I should have a look at the actual member.

EUGENE: What?

DR. FLIM: The member. You know.

EUGENE: I don't understand.

DR. FLIM: It says here that you have a small member.

EUGENE: A small member?

DR. FLIM: That's right. That you're suffering from feelings of inadequacy caused by the size of your "freakishly small member." "Almost microscopic," it says. I'm sure that's an exaggeration.

EUGENE: *[Horrified.]* No! I mean, yes! Yes! It is an exaggeration! I mean, it's not an exaggeration because I never said that at all! It's not true! Any of it!

DR. FLIM: No?

EUGENE: No!

DR. FLIM: You don't have a small member?

EUGENE: Not small! I mean, maybe not large, but ... at least average! I have a very average member! I mean, it's certainly not a problem!

DR. FLIM: Hmmm ... I wonder why she would have written that?

EUGENE: I have no idea! I mean, all right, I'll be honest—I did get the impression she didn't like me very much.

DR. FLIM: Well, I'm sure she wouldn't allow that to interfere with her professional evaluation. Perhaps she misunderstood.

EUGENE: I don't see how that's possible.

DR. FLIM: So there's no problem with your—

EUGENE: No! None whatsoever!

DR. FLIM: Would you like me to take a look—just in case?

EUGENE: I don't think that's necessary.

DR. FLIM: Just a quick peek? For good measure?

EUGENE: Really—I'm fine.

DR. FLIM: All right. What's the problem then?

EUGENE: Spots. I've got spots.

DR. FLIM: On your—

EUGENE: Everywhere! And they itch! They're very itchy! At night I have to wear a muzzle!
> *[Again, EUGENE offers his arm. DR. FLIM studies it carefully.]*

DR. FLIM: Do you have a temperature?

EUGENE: No. No temperature.

DR. FLIM: Hmmm ...

EUGENE: What? Is it bad? *[DR. FLIM continues to study EUGENE.]* Am I going to die? Oh god! I'm going to die—right?! I read in the paper about a flesh-eating virus that devoured a man in a matter of hours, and I knew, somewhere inside, I knew that if something like that really existed, I was bound to catch it! This is just my luck!

DR. FLIM: I'll be honest with you—I've never seen anything like this before. It's a bit unusual. It could be stress-related. Or some sort of terrorist plague.

EUGENE: Terrorist plague?!

DR. FLIM: Probably stress.

EUGENE: You said terrorist plague!

DR. FLIM: I was only joking. I'm sure it's nothing a little rest and relaxation won't cure.

EUGENE: So it is stress then?

DR. FLIM: That would be my guess. We'll run a few tests just to be sure. I'll have Margo take some blood. I'm also going to have my partner take a look, if you don't mind. But I'm sure it's nothing to worry about.

EUGENE: But ... the thing is ... my main source of stress is these spots! Before the spots, I had very little stress! No stress at all, really! Normally, I'm very relaxed! Water off the back—all that! You can ask my wife if you don't—oh! I almost forgot! Did Margo ask about my wife?

DR. FLIM: No. Does she have spots too?

EUGENE: No, I asked if it might be possible for her to wait in here with me. In the examining room.

DR. FLIM: She didn't mention that.

EUGENE: It's just that I'm a little nervous, you know, and she tends to have a—

DR. FLIM: I should think that would be fine.

EUGENE: She's in the lobby. She's wearing a green dress with flowers and a little hat that—

DR. FLIM: I'll have Margo fetch her for you.

EUGENE: Thank you.
        [DR. FLIM nods and exits. EUGENE sits for a moment, looks at his watch, then picks up a magazine and begins to read. After a moment, the NURSE enters, glaring. She slams the door behind her and locks it. In her hands, she holds a needle and syringe.]

NURSE: What is WRONG with you?! Are you trying to get me FIRED?!

EUGENE: What? I ... no!

NURSE: How could you question my authority like that?!

EUGENE: I ... I didn't mean to—

NURSE: Do you think this job means nothing to me?! Do you think I won't fight to protect it?!
        [She approaches him with the needle and syringe.]

EUGENE: *[Rising.]* Okay, maybe I should—

NURSE: SIT! *[EUGENE sits.]* Give me your arm!

EUGENE: I don't know if that's such a—

NURSE: Your ARM!
        [Reluctantly, he complies. She ties a rubber tourniquet around his arm and roughly inserts the needle.]

EUGENE: Ow! Owww! Careful with that thing!
        [The syringe begins to fill with blood.]

NURSE: You realize with one little twist of this needle I could tear your vein in half?

EUGENE: Please don't.

NURSE: Or I could reverse the flow—send an air bubble straight to your brain—no one would ever suspect it was anything but a terrible accident.

EUGENE: Help!

NURSE: Shut up!

EUGENE: All right!

NURSE: Listen to me when I'm talking!

EUGENE: I'm listening!

NURSE: I don't think you are!

EUGENE: I am! I swear! See! *[He listens.]*

NURSE: I don't like to be reprimanded! That bitch questioned my integrity! Do you know what that's like?! To have your integrity questioned?!

EUGENE: Yes! Yes! It happens to me all the time!

NURSE: Don't make fun of me!

EUGENE: I'm not!

NURSE: Why couldn't you just play along?!

EUGENE: She ... she wanted to see my member!

NURSE: She threatened me with my JOB! My LIVELIHOOD!

EUGENE: I'm sorry! I don't know what I was thinking! It won't happen again!
    [The NURSE studies EUGENE for a moment.]

NURSE: All right ... I'm going to let you live.

EUGENE: Thank you! Thank you!

NURSE: But you owe me.
    [She removes the needle from EUGENE'S arm.]

EUGENE: How much blood did you take? I feel faint.

NURSE: Don't be such a baby. *[She applies a bandage.]* There—all better.

EUGENE: It still hurts.

NURSE: Do you want me to kiss it?

EUGENE: No.

NURSE: Well, don't say I didn't offer.
    [She gathers the blood samples and turns to go.]

EUGENE: Oh, by the way, the doctor said my wife could come back.

NURSE: *[Sharply.]* I know what the doctor said.

EUGENE: All right. I'm just–
    *[The NURSE exits. Almost immediately, DR. FLAM enters.
    She looks exactly like DR. FLIM except that she wears a
    brightly-colored clown wig.]*

DR. FLAM: Hello. I'm Dr. Flam.

EUGENE: You mean Flim.

DR. FLAM: No, Flam.

EUGENE: But before you—

DR. FLAM: Before?

EUGENE: Yes. When you were here before—

DR. FLAM: Oh, that was Dr. Flim—my partner. She asked me to take a look at you.

EUGENE: Oh. You look exactly alike. I mean, except for the wig.

DR. FLAM: What wig?

EUGENE: That one. The one you're wearing.

DR. FLAM: This is my natural hair. Do you like it?

EUGENE: It's … it's lovely.

DR. FLAM: Well, let's take a look. *[EUGENE offers his arm.]* Hmmm … just as I suspected.

EUGENE: What is it?

DR. FLAM: I have no idea. But I suspected as much, so it's really no surprise. What you need is a specialist.

EUGENE: A specialist?

DR. FLAM: That's right. Someone who's devoted his life to studying this sort of thing. And I know just the man. He's a genius. A real giant among men. His knowledge of spots is encyclopedic—almost inhuman. Godlike, if you will. They say he's even performed a few miracles. Miracle cures, you know. He will, no doubt, diagnose your illness in the blink of an eye.

EUGENE: When can I see him?

DR. FLAM: Never. He's booked for years in advance, decades—well into the next millennium. *[EUGENE is speechless. She laughs.]* I'm kidding! He's one floor up. I'll see if he can swing down and take a look.

EUGENE: Thank you! Thank you! That would be great! *[She nods and moves to the door.]* Oh! There's one more thing. The nurse was supposed to send my wife in.

DR. FLAM: Margo? She's completely incompetent. A real nutcase. We only keep her on because Dr. Flim has a thing for her.

EUGENE: Do you think you could send her back?

DR. FLAM: Margo?

EUGENE: No—my wife.

DR. FLAM: Of course. Where is she?

EUGENE: The lobby.

DR. FLAM: *[With a grimace.]* Oooh … that's too bad.

EUGENE: What do you mean? *[Pause.]* What? What is it?!
[Pause.]

DR. FLAM: Well … I probably shouldn't tell you this, but … the
lobby is under quarantine. There's been some kind of outbreak.

EUGENE: An outbreak?! What … what kind of outbreak?!

DR. FLAM: We don't have all the details yet.

EUGENE: Is it serious?!

DR. FLAM: Something about a plague.

EUGENE: A plague?! In the lobby?! My god!

DR. FLAM: I'm sure it's nothing to worry about. *[EUGENE moves
to the door. She blocks his path.]* Where do you think you're going?

EUGENE: I have to see my wife.

DR. FLAM: Sir, you need to sit down and let the professionals handle
this.

EUGENE: But—

DR. FLAM: I'm sure your wife is fine. So far it's just the old and very young who are actually dying. And a few sickly teenagers. Your wife isn't a teenager, is she?

EUGENE: No.

DR. FLAM: Then you have nothing to worry about. Just have a seat while I place that call to the Specialist, and I'll have someone check on your wife. All right?

EUGENE: *[Hesitates.]* Okay. Thank you.
    [DR. FLAM exits. EUGENE sits in dazed silence. A moment later, DR. FLIM returns wearing a hospital mask.]

DR. FLIM: It doesn't exist!

EUGENE: What?

DR. FLIM: Your disease! I've been through all the medical books! Every database! It just doesn't exist! There's no such thing!

EUGENE: But ... surely in one of your textbooks ... somewhere ... I mean, there ... there must be some reference! I can't be the first person ever to have this problem!

DR. FLIM: Every plague starts with one person.

EUGENE: This is just my luck!

DR. FLIM: One little mutated cell. One bad seed.

EUGENE: Wait—you're ... you're saying the plague in the lobby, the quarantine, it's ... it's all my fault?!

DR. FLIM: It's not just the lobby. The whole building's under quarantine.

EUGENE: The whole building? Good lord! And ... people are actually dying?!

DR. FLIM: They're dropping like flies.

EUGENE: What about the Specialist? Has he come yet?

DR. FLIM: What specialist?

EUGENE: The Specialist. One floor up. The one Dr. Flam—

DR. FLIM: Him? Ha! He's a quack! Some guy she used to bone in college!

EUGENE: But ... she said he was a genius.

DR. FLIM: Pfff!

EUGENE: She said he could perform miracles.

DR. FLIM: He's a drooling idiot!

EUGENE: So, he ... he's not ...

DR. FLIM: He's not even certified.

EUGENE: Then ... there's no hope.

DR. FLIM: Not really.

EUGENE: We're all going to die.

DR. FLIM: That's the most likely outcome. Yes.

EUGENE: And it's all my fault.

DR. FLIM: No, no, not at all. *[Pause.]* Okay, yes it is. I can't lie.

EUGENE: I want to see my wife.

DR. FLIM: I told Margo to send her back. Hasn't she come?

EUGENE: No.

DR. FLIM: That woman! If she wasn't so damned attractive, I'd fire her on the spot!
 [DR. FLIM exits. A moment later, the NURSE bursts into the room.]

NURSE: Is it true?! Have they sent for the Specialist?!

EUGENE: Well ... yes.

NURSE: Finally! After all these years!

EUGENE: But ... Dr. Flim said he's a quack.

NURSE: She's jealous!

EUGENE: He isn't even certified.

NURSE: They're ALL jealous! He's so far beyond them, they can't comprehend his tiniest thought! And you! You're responsible for bringing him here! I could kiss you! I could do more than that, if you'd like!
 [She tries to kiss him.]

EUGENE: What ... what are you doing?!

NURSE: Don't you find me attractive? Don't you want me— sexually, I mean?

EUGENE: Well, I ...

NURSE: What about these? Do you like these?
 [She shows EUGENE her breasts.]

EUGENE: Well, I ... they're ... they're very ... ahh ... nice, but—

NURSE: Nice?

EUGENE: Yes.

NURSE: Just nice?

EUGENE: I ... I really don't—

NURSE: You want to touch them?

EUGENE: What?

NURSE: Go ahead. No one's watching. The world's coming to an end. You might as well.

EUGENE: Shouldn't you be working? I mean, I'm sure they need your help—with the building under quarantine and all.

NURSE: Oh, it's not just the building. The whole city's under quarantine.

EUGENE: The whole city?!

NURSE: That's right. And it won't stop there. The country. The world. Society's falling apart—civilization as we know it. It's unraveling. The thread has been pulled. Everyone's dying. Survivors are running for the hills. Hiding in caves. There's no food. People are eating their own children.

EUGENE: My God!

NURSE: We're going the way of the dinosaurs. It was only a matter of time.

EUGENE: I want to see my wife! Right now! The doctor told you to send her back!

NURSE: How can you think of your wife at a time like this?

EUGENE: Who else should I think of?

NURSE: *[Covering her breasts.]* Oh, fine.

EUGENE: She's wearing a—

NURSE: I know! I know! A green dress with flowers!

EUGENE: And a hat that—
[*The NURSE exits in a huff and returns a moment later, wearing a hat and a green dress with flowers.*]

NURSE: Hello, darling.
[She kisses him.]

EUGENE: What … what are you doing?! Why are you wearing my wife's clothes?!

NURSE: Sweetheart—what are you talking about? Don't you know your own wife?

EUGENE: You're not my wife!

NURSE: Of course I am. Those spots must have gone to your brain.

EUGENE: *[Shaking her violently.]* No! No! I'm not crazy! Where is she?! What have you done with her?!

NURSE: Sweetheart, I—

EUGENE: What have you done with my wife?!

NURSE: Why don't we just go home and—

EUGENE: TELL ME!!! *[Pause.]*

NURSE: All right, fine. Have it your way. *[She removes the hat.]* She's dead.

EUGENE: What? You're … you're lying!

NURSE: No, she was one of the first to go.
      [EUGENE releases her. He backs away.]

EUGENE: This can't be happening.

NURSE: She was weak—no will to live.

EUGENE: I want to see the body.

NURSE: Too late. It's already been burned—to stop the spread of the disease, you know.

EUGENE: Oh God! What have I done! I've killed my own wife! I've given her my disease!

NURSE: Don't be such a crybaby! My god! Here you are, at the end of the world, with a drop-dead gorgeous horny nurse practically throwing herself at you—some men would consider this a fantasy come true.

EUGENE: But my wife—

NURSE: Shut up about your wife! Stop living in the past!

EUGENE: How can you—

NURSE: For god's sake! Take me!

EUGENE: But—

NURSE: Take me! Right here! On this table! Give me your disease!

EUGENE: You ... you want my disease?

NURSE: Yes! I want it! I want to taste death! I want to feel its weight pressing down on me—the weight of a dying man! I want to hear its soft whisper! Its anguished cry! I want to take it inside me like a child! Nurture it! Let it grow! Let it feed on me like a sack of rice! And then, finally, open myself up ... unleash it upon the world ... a great sweaty monster of spotted flesh and stinking bodies!

EUGENE: You're insane!
[She kisses EUGENE. He struggles, but she clings to him passionately. There is a clawing sound at the door.]

EUGENE: What's that?

NURSE: Nothing! Kiss me!
[Again, a clawing sound at the door. EUGENE pulls away.]

EUGENE: It might be the Specialist! Maybe there's still time!
[EUGENE opens the door, and THE SPECIALIST lumbers into the room. He is a sub-human creature, a throwback to the age of the Neanderthal, an idiot-retard who cannot speak but only drools and grunts. He is dressed, however, like a distinguished physician.]
This ... this can't be him!
[The SPECIALIST grunts.]

NURSE: Of course it is! Who else would it be?
[She takes the SPECIALIST by the arm and leads him to the rolling stool. He sits, as if upon a throne, and grunts his approval.]

EUGENE: What's wrong with him? *[To the SPECIALIST.]* Have you been in some kind of accident?

NURSE: Don't talk to him that way! He's a genius! *[She strokes the SPECIALIST'S hair. He grunts with pleasure.]* Oh, look—he likes that!

EUGENE: He ... he can't really be the great doctor—can he? The pinnacle of man's learning? Is it possible this is all we amount to? *[To the SPECIALIST.]* Can you understand me? Are you insane? Or ... no! Perhaps ... perhaps I'm insane! That's it! You're speaking normally, but I can't understand because I've finally lost my mind! Or ... or perhaps we're both insane! Both trying desperately to communicate but—
> *[The SPECIALIST sniffs under the NURSE's skirt.]*

NURSE: Oh! You're so naughty!
> *[The SPECIALIST and the NURSE perform the carnal act.]*

EUGENE: What are you doing? Don't do that!

NURSE: Yes! Oh, yes! I can feel your enlightenment pouring into me! Your knowledge!

EUGENE: Stop it! Stop! For god's sake, she's ... she's wearing my wife's dress! *[EUGENE picks up the doctor's stool and brandishes it like a weapon.]* I won't allow this! I forbid you to continue! Do you hear me?! Stop! I ... I said stop!
> *[The SPECIALIST grunts in ecstasy. EUGENE begins to pummel him with the chair.]*

NURSE: What are you doing?! Don't hurt him! Leave him alone! *[There is a struggle, but soon the SPECIALIST lies dead. EUGENE throws the chair to the ground.]* What have you done?! He was our only hope!
> *[She lunges at EUGENE and begins to pound him with her fists.]*

EUGENE: Don't! Please! I ... I don't want to hurt you!

NURSE: Help! Murder!

EUGENE: Shhh! Be quiet!

NURSE: Murder!

[EUGENE grabs her by the throat. He holds the NURSE until she, too, lies motionless. EUGENE hovers over her for a moment, breathing heavily—then backs away, horrified.]

EUGENE: Oh God! *[There is a knock at the door. EUGENE freezes, tries to regain his composure.]* Who ... who is it? Who's there?

VOICE: *[Offstage.]* The Specialist. *[Blackout.]*

* * *

FAMILY 2.0

Family 2.0 was originally produced on April 6, 2007, by La Cosa Nostra Productions in Tallahassee, Florida. The production was directed by Seth Federman. The cast was as follows:

WIFE: Rebecca Marchetti
HUSBAND: Kevin Sullivan
SON: Danielle Festa
DAUGHTER: Katerina Gawlak
FIRST HUSBAND/DOG: Jared Hair

SETTING:
A perfect-looking house—the kind you find in magazines.

[A perfect-looking house—the kind you find in magazines. A perfect-looking WIFE puts the finishing touches on her perfect-looking living room. The front door opens and HUSBAND enters.]

HUSBAND: Hi, Honey! I'm home!

WIFE: Who are you? What are you doing in my house?!

HUSBAND: I'm your new husband. Where should I put my coat? *[He tries to kiss WIFE, but she backs away from him terrified.]*

WIFE: Don't touch me! I'll scream! I'll call the police!

HUSBAND: Aren't you going to ask how my day was?

WIFE: *[Attempting to pacify him.]* How ... how was your day?

HUSBAND: It was awful! Just like every other day! Same old boring job. Same old boring boss. Same old boring life. And then, on the way home, suddenly it hit me—why come home to the same old boring wife and house and kids and dog when I could try something new?

WIFE: But you can't just—

HUSBAND: I've always admired your home. It's very well kept.

WIFE: Thank you, but—

HUSBAND: I pass it every day on my way to work, so I thought today I'd give it a try. It has to be more exciting than the one I've been coming home to for the past fifteen years.

WIFE: But ... I already have a husband.

HUSBAND: He can have my life. Where does he work?

55

WIFE: He's an executive. At a technology company.

HUSBAND: Perfect! I love technology! All those little gadgets and stuff! It'll be great!

WIFE: Look, I'm … I'm sorry your life is so boring. My life is boring too. But you can't just walk in here and expect us to—

HUSBAND: Oh! I almost forgot! I brought you flowers!
    [He produces a bouquet of flowers from his coat.]

WIFE: You brought me flowers?

HUSBAND: They're orchids—a symbol of rare beauty and eternal love—my love for you.

WIFE: My … my husband hasn't brought me flowers in almost fifteen years.

HUSBAND: I wrote you a poem too.

WIFE: A poem?

HUSBAND: Would you like me to recite it?

WIFE: Well … if you went to the trouble of writing it … I … I wouldn't want it to go to waste.

HUSBAND: You take my breath away.
Like the sunset or a summer day.
When I gaze at the moon
Or the ocean blue
They pale beside the sight of you.
You take my breath away.

WIFE: That's beautiful. You … you really wrote that?

HUSBAND: For you.

[Pause. She considers this.]

WIFE: Do you pee in the shower?

HUSBAND: Never.

WIFE: Hog the sheets?

HUSBAND: Nope.

WIFE: Snore?

HUSBAND: I don't think so.

WIFE: Any history of baldness in your family?

HUSBAND: On the contrary. We're very hairy.

WIFE: Would you do your own laundry or wait for me to do it.

HUSBAND: Do it myself.

WIFE: Fix the toilet or call a plumber?

HUSBAND: Fix it.

WIFE: Shingle the roof or buy a new house?

HUSBAND: New house.

WIFE: Anniversary in Maui or Vegas?

HUSBAND: Maui.

WIFE: Watch football or do me in the kitchen?

HUSBAND: Do you really have to ask?

WIFE: Will you constantly try to pork me in the rear?

HUSBAND: Only if you want me to.

WIFE: Tell me about your first wife.

HUSBAND: She was a nag. A nag with no boobs. She had boobs until the baby was born, but he sucked them right off. I'm a boob man, so it was completely unworkable.

WIFE: You left because she lost her boobs?

HUSBAND: There were other things. But I have to be honest—it was mainly the boobs.

WIFE: What if I lose my boobs? Will you leave me too?

HUSBAND: It looks like you've got plenty to spare! *[They make out.]* Can we have sex now?

WIFE: Easy, Tiger. You'll have to win the kids over first. Children! *[Enter SON and DAUGHTER.]* Children, meet your new father.

HUSBAND: Hi, kids.

SON: You're not my father! You're a fake! An imposter!

HUSBAND: Do you like baseball?

SON: Sure.

HUSBAND: I'll take you to the Big Game.

SON: The Big Game?! No way! *[He embraces HUSBAND.]* I love you, Dad!

DAUGHTER: What about me? I hate baseball.

HUSBAND: Do you like shopping?

DAUGHTER: Duh.

HUSBAND: Here—knock yourself out.
      [He hands her a hundred dollar bill.]

DAUGHTER: A hundred dollar bill?! You're the greatest!
      [She kisses HUSBAND on the cheek.]

WIFE: Go play in your room, kids. Your father and I need some time alone.

DAUGHTER: Sure thing, Mom.

SON: See ya later, Dad.
      [Exit kids.]

WIFE: *[Seductively.]* Now where were we?
      [They make out. Enter FIRST HUSBAND.]

FIRST HUSBAND: Hi, Honey! I'm ... what's going on here?! What are you doing to my wife?!

HUSBAND: I'm trying to pork her in the rear.

FIRST HUSBAND: I'm calling the police!

WIFE: Wait! Give me your key.

FIRST HUSBAND: What?

WIFE: Your key. Hand it over.

FIRST HUSBAND: I don't understand.

WIFE: He's replacing you.

FIRST HUSBAND: Replacing me?

WIFE: That's right. He's in—you're out.

FIRST HUSBAND: But why?!

WIFE: He brought me flowers! When's the last time you brought me flowers?!

FIRST HUSBAND: I—

WIFE: Exactly. Now stop stuttering and hand over the key.

FIRST HUSBAND: But … what about the kids?! You can't take the kids away from me! Kids! *[Enter SON and DAUGHTER.]* You don't want me to go—do you kids?

SON: He's taking me to the Big Game.

FIRST HUSBAND: I'll take you!

SON: Too late. You had your chance.

FIRST HUSBAND: But—

DAUGHTER: Sorry. It's nothing personal.

WIFE: *[Her hand outstretched.]* The key.

FIRST HUSBAND: But I don't want to go! Please, I'll … I'll do anything! Just let me stay! I won't bother you! I'll stay out of the way! I'll … I'll be another kid! Or the family dog!

SON: I've always wanted a dog!

DAUGHTER: Eww! He's gonna get hair everywhere!

SON: Please?! Can I keep him?! Can I?!

WIFE: I don't know. What do you think, Honey?

HUSBAND: He'd be your responsibility, Son. We're not going to feed him for you, or take him for walks, or clean up his poop—

SON: I'll take care of him! I promise! *[To FIRST HUSBAND/DOG.]* Come here, boy! Sit! Roll over! Play dead! Good boy!

FIRST HUSBAND/DOG: Woof! Woof!

DAUGHTER: Can I go shopping now?

WIFE: If your father will drive you.

DAUGHTER: Dad?

HUSBAND: Well … your mother and I were sort of in the middle of something.

DAUGHTER: But I want to go now! There's a sale!

FIRST HUSBAND/DOG: Woof! Woof!

HUSBAND: Okay, just give us—

FIRST HUSBAND/DOG: Woof!

WIFE: I think the dog has to go.

HUSBAND: Son, take your dog outside.

SON: I can't. I have homework.
     [Exit SON.]

DAUGHTER: Can I go shopping or not?

FIRST HUSBAND/DOG: Woof! Woof!

WIFE: Honey, could you take care of the dog?

HUSBAND: It's not my dog.

WIFE: You told him he could keep it.

FIRST HUSBAND/DOG: Woof!

HUSBAND: Do we have a leash?

DAUGHTER: Is anybody listening to me?
    [Enter SON with baseball and glove.]

SON: Hey Dad, can we play ball?

HUSBAND: I thought you had homework.

SON: I just finished.

DAUGHTER: Hello?

FIRST HUSBAND/DOG: Woof! Woof!

HUSBAND: *[To SON.]* Here—take the dog outside.

SON: I have to poop.
    [Exit SON.]

WIFE: *[To HUSBAND]* While you're out, can you take the trash?

FIRST HUSBAND/DOG: Woof!

HUSBAND: Ahh … sure.

DAUGHTER: I hate this family!

WIFE: And could you do something about your daughter?

FIRST HUSBAND/DOG: Woof!

HUSBAND: What do you want me to—

FIRST HUSBAND/DOG: Woof! Woof!

HUSBAND: *[To FIRST HUSBAND/DOG]* Shut up, you stupid mutt!

FIRST HUSBAND/DOG: Grrr!
        *[FIRST HUSBAND/DOG bites HUSBAND'S pants and pulls
        him towards the door.]*

WIFE: I think he really wants to go.

DAUGHTER: What about me?! Does anybody care what I want?!
        [Enter SON.]

SON: The Big Game starts any minute! We have to go!

HUSBAND: *[To WIFE]* When ... when we get back it would be
really nice to have some quality alone time if you know what I mean.

WIFE: It'll have to wait, Dear. You have responsibilities now.

HUSBAND: Responsibilities?! This isn't what I signed up for!
You're just like my first wife!

WIFE: WHAT did you say?!!!

HUSBAND: I—

WIFE: Don't compare me to that flat-chested bitch!

HUSBAND: I didn't mean—

WIFE: Do you see these tits?! Do you ever want to touch these tits
again?!

HUSBAND: Yes! Yes, I do! That's what I—

FIRST HUSBAND/DOG: Woof! Woof!

SON: We're gonna miss the game! We have to go NOW!

DAUGHTER: I asked first! It's not fair!

WIFE: If I ever hear you even THINK her name again—

DAUGHTER: You can't just ignore me!

SON: You promised!

WIFE: I swear to God—

FIRST HUSBAND/DOG: Woof!
> [As the cacophony rises, everyone converges on HUSBAND who climbs onto the couch to escape them. They surround him like a pack of rabid wolves.]

WIFE	SON	DAUGHTER	DOG
Your balls will	All I wanted to	Am I invisible?	Woof!
be so blue you'll	do was go to	Am I not even	Woof!
be begging me	the Big Game!	here? What do I	Woof!
to fuck *you* in	But now it's	have to do to get	Woof!
the ass! Are you	too late! I	some attention in	Woof!
hearing me?!	already told all	this house?! Do	Woof!
Are we clear on	of my friends	I have to shoot	Woof!
this?! It's gonna	we were	somebody? Do I	Woof!
take a LOT of	going, and	have to blow	Woof!
ass-kissing to	they're all	something up?	Woof!
make up for this	going too, and	Maybe I should	Woof!
little slip-up,	now they're	get pregnant! I	Woof!
Mister! Not	going to see	should find the	Woof!
only am I not	that I'm not	first boy who	Woof!
like her, but she	really there	wants to fuck me	Woof!
doesn't exist!	and they're	and just pull up	Woof!

She's a figment of your imagination! She's not even a figment! I am the first and *only* woman you've ever loved, buddy, and you will grovel at my feet if you want any pudding from my kitchen! going to know what losers we are! I'll bet you didn't even buy tickets—did you?! Liar! My other Dad would have taken me! I should have gone with him! I'm never going to believe another word you say! You're a big fat ugly liar! my skirt! There are plenty of boys at school who'd like to fuck me! Maybe they already have! Maybe I just haven't told you! Or maybe I have but you don't fucking listen! Woof! Woof! Woof! Woof! Woof! Woof! Woof! Woof! Woof! Woof! Woof! Woof! Woof! Woof! Woof! Woof! Woof! Woof! Woof!

HUSBAND: I NEED A NEW LIFE!!!
   [Blackout.]

* * *

THE TRAGICAL TALE OF MELISSA McHINEY McNORMOUS McWHALE

The Tragical Tale of Melissa McHiney McNormous McWhale was originally produced on June 14, 2008, by the Kununurra Amateur Theatre Society in Kununurra, Australia. The production was directed by Carolyn Maskiell.

MELISSA
CHORUS #1
CHORUS #2
CHORUS #3
BROTHER #1
BROTHER #2
BROTHER #3
SPECTATOR #1
SPECTATOR #2
SPECTATOR #3
STRANGER
MARVIN

NOTE: Actors can and should play multiple roles.

SETTING:
Las Vegas, Nevada.

[Lights up on CHORUS. Each chorus member should be dressed as some sort of traditional Las Vegas character—a lounge lizard, a mobster, a showgirl, an Elvis impersonator...]

CHORUS #1: Welcome, my friends, to the city of lights!

CHORUS #2: The city of showgirls and heavyweight fights!

CHORUS #3: The city of blackjack!

CHORUS #2: Love for sale!

CHORUS #1: And Melissa McHiney McNormous McWhale!
[Lights up on MELISSA—an otherwise attractive woman with a grotesquely large buttocks.]

CHORUS #3: Melissa was different, and this is no jive—

CHORUS #2: Her measurements: 36-22-85!

CHORUS #1: Yes, her bottom was sizably larger than others.

CHORUS #2: It was two times the size of all six of her brothers.

BROTHER #1: Fat-ass!

BROTHER #2: Jelly-butt!

BROTHER #3: Dinosaur!

BROTHER #1: Freak!

CHORUS #3: She was somewhat ashamed of her strange-shaped physique.

CHORUS #1: Until one day, in her oversized Prada,

CHORUS #2: She stumbled upon Las Vegas, Nevada—

CHORUS #1: A city where oddities don't make you lame,

CHORUS #3: But instead bring you riches and fortune and fame.

CHORUS #2: Step right up, folks! It'd be quite a blunder
To miss out on this physiological wonder!
Feast your eyes, if you will, on the curious tail
Of Melissa McHiney McNormous McWhale!

SPECTATOR #1: My god! She's enormous!

SPECTATOR #2: How'd they get her inside?!

SPECTATOR #3: It must be a fake! No one's butt is that wide!

CHORUS #1: They gaped and they ogled.

CHORUS #2: They came every night.

CHORUS #3: When she wiggled her bottom they'd squeal with delight.

SPECTATOR #3: Did you see how it jiggled?!

SPECTATOR #1: It gives me the shivers!

SPECTATOR #2: It's the rippling effect where she really delivers!

CHORUS #1: She was quite the sensation.

CHORUS #2: No longer a chump.

CHORUS #3: And all on account of her ginormous rump!

CHORUS #1: They put her on billboards!

CHORUS #2: Celebrity panels!

CHORUS #1: On magazine covers!

CHORUS #2: The Gambling Channel!

CHORUS #3: On the Strip they erected a fifty-foot statue
With an ass that appeared to be coming right at you!

CHORUS #2: It was fitted with thousands of big neon lights.

CHORUS #1: So it lit up the city on the darkest of nights.

CHORUS #3: But in spite of the fanfare and parties they'd thrown
Deep inside, Melissa still felt quite alone.

CHORUS #2: Then one fateful night, a strange-looking joe
Slipped into her dressing room after a show.

MELISSA: Who are you?

STRANGER: Don't be frightened. I've come to correct
Your terrible monstrous ginormous defect!

MELISSA: My defect?

STRANGER: Your backside! Your deformed hindquarter!
With my skills I can make it considerably shorter!

MELISSA: But people here love me. They built me a statue.

STRANGER: That statue is only intended to mock you!
Can't you see you're a monster! A freakish mutation!

MELISSA: Go away!

STRANGER: Not until I have offered salvation!
I can fix you. You see, I'm a world-renowned surgeon.
My name is Dr. Sylvester McPurgeon.
I can take your deformity—cut it just so

And voila! You'll look just like Bridgette Bardot!
Here's my card. You may call any time, night or day.

CHORUS #3: And with that good doctor scampered away.

CHORUS #1: That night, as Melissa tossed in her bed,
McPurgeon's cruel words danced around in her head.

STRANGER: Can't you see you're a monster! A freakish mutation!

MELISSA: He's right! I'll try the proposed amputation!

CHORUS #2: That morning, she took the first bus of the day—

CHORUS #3: To go see the surgeon and lose her boo-tay.

CHORUS #1: But as Fate would have it—

CHORUS #2: And Fate rules this town.

CHORUS #3: On this very bus sat Marvin the Clown.

MARVIN: Howdy doo! How ya doing? Do ya ride the bus often?

CHORUS #1: And right away her resolve started to soften.

CHORUS #3: For Marvin, like her, had an uncommon trait.

MELISSA: Your feet …

CHORUS #2: They were large.

CHORUS #1: They were size ninety-eight.

MARVIN: Yes, my feet are gigantic.

MELISSA: They match my rear-end.

MARVIN: I believe we are destined to be more than friends.

CHORUS #3: That very day, they became man and wife.

CHORUS #1: They found a small chapel and bonded for life.

CHORUS #2: Overseeing the service was a big, sweaty Elvis

CHORUS #1: Who crooned their vows while shaking his pelvis.

CHORUS #3: [As ELVIS, shaking pelvis.] Love her tender! Love her true!

MARVIN: I do.

MELISSA: So do I.

CHORUS #3: [As ELVIS, shaking pelvis.] Well, then kiss her, you fool!

CHORUS #1: Yes, Melissa had finally found her soul mate.

CHORUS #2: They booked a room at the Luxor and began to procreate.

CHORUS #3: And it turns out Melissa was in for a treat.

MARVIN: 'Cause you know what they say about men with big feet!

CHORUS #1: Melissa and Marvin had kids of all sizes—

CHORUS #2: With gargantuan noses and humongous eyeses.

CHORUS #3: With fingers that stretched right up to the stars!

CHORUS #2: And breasts that were larger than many small cars!

CHORUS #1: Some could read minds!

CHORUS #3: Some could dance unsurpassed!

CHORUS #2: And one could pull doves right out of his … … … hat.

CHORUS #1: They filled the Strip with so many strange forms
That oversized body parts soon were the norm.

CHORUS #3: And those who'd made normal such a priority
Were now the dully symmetric minority.

SPECTATOR #2: My butt is so small!

SPECTATOR #3: I can't make it jiggle!

SPECTATOR #1: If only I had just a little more wiggle!

CHORUS #2: Melissa and Marvin had conquered the town.

CHORUS #3: Their progeny thrived and earned them renown.

CHORUS #1: Then one day they vanished—

CHORUS #2: Just dropped out of sight.

CHORUS #3: No one knows where they went—

CHORUS #1: Or if they're all right.

CHORUS #3: But according to rumor, they went to Groom Lake—

CHORUS #2: Were mistaken for aliens and shot by mistake.

CHORUS #1: We hope it's not true.

CHORUS #2: But you never can tell.

CHORUS #3: In Las Vegas, nothing ends very well.

CHORUS #2: And that, my friends, is the tragical tale

CHORUS #1: Of Melissa McHiney McNormous McWhale.

* * *

CHERRY BIZARRE

An homage to Anton Chekhov's *The Cherry Orchard*

Cherry Bizarre was originally produced on April 25, 1997 by Poor Playwrights' Theatre in Las Vegas, Nevada. The production was directed by Mary Geerlof. The cast was as follows:

LOPAHIN: Scott Johnson
EPIHODOV: Russ Marchand
GAEV: Larry Dwyer
FIRS: Matthew Sorvillo

SETTING:
A small, country store.

[A small country store. LOPAHIN, a merchant, rests on a stool behind the counter. FIRS, an old man, mumbles incoherently to himself as he sweeps up. There are crates of cherries everywhere and a sign which reads "Cherries for Sale...CHEAP!"]

LOPAHIN: You're a good worker Firs, old man. I don't know how I ever got along without you. You've been quite helpful this past year. Very helpful indeed. You've missed a spot. Very good. Thank you, Firs. *[FIRS says something, but not a word can be distinguished.]* I remember when I was a lad of fifteen, I used to sweep up for my father—he kept a little shop in those days. One day, I missed a spot. Father was furious. I'll never forget that day. He took a broom and shoved it up my ass. Right up my ass! I remember quite clearly.
    [Enter GAEV. He rushes to the counter.]

GAEV: Lopahin! I must speak with you! It's urgent!

LOPAHIN: Not now—I'm in the middle of a story.

GAEV: But it's urgent!

LOPAHIN: Where was I? *[FIRS mumbles.]* That's right—the broom!

GAEV: *[Spots an empty bookcase.]* Ah! There you are! *[Rushes to the bookcase.]* Oh! Beloved friend! Don't worry, I'll get you out of here! Lopahin, how much do you want for this bookcase?

LOPAHIN: In a moment.

GAEV: Name your price!

LOPAHIN: Where was I? It's so hard to remember after one is interrupted! Oh, yes!

GAEV: *[To the bookcase.]* Are you well, my friend? Oh, dearest bookcase! Faithful companion! How I've missed you! You mustn't

79

hate me for leaving. I always intended to come back for you! You must believe that!
> *[A large pile of cherry crates crashes to the floor as EPIHODOV enters. Cherries fly everywhere. FIRS mumbles something and begins sweeping them up.]*

EPIHODOV: Sorry, everyone! Sorry! Don't mind me. Every day some misfortune befalls me. I don't complain. I'm used to it, and I wear a smiling face!

LOPAHIN: Ah! Good Epihodov! I remember, when I was fifteen I once knocked over a crate of cherries in my father's store. I remember quite vividly. He took the crate and shoved it up my ass. Right up my ass! I was shitting splinters for weeks!
> *[EPIHODOV trips over his own feet and crashes into the counter, splitting his head open.]*

EPIHODOV: There! There, you see! I've split my head open! How do you like that?!

LOPAHIN: The usual?

EPIHODOV: Yes, and a few extra bandages this week if you don't mind.

LOPAHIN: Certainly, my friend!

GAEV: [To the bookshelf.] Friend? Friend?! Hah! They know nothing of friendship! You and I—we know of friendship! Always true! Never faltering! No, no ... don't cry. Hush now, little bookcase. *[Sotto voce.]* Don't worry ... I have a plan to get you out of here! Shhh! They'll hear you!
> *[LOPAHIN hands EPIHODOV a box of bandages.]*

LOPAHIN: Bandages, there you go. Anything else?

EPIHODOV: Perhaps a little extra gauze? And some kind of disinfectant for minor cuts and bruises?

LOPAHIN: Of course. *[LOPAHIN hands EPIHODOV a long strip of wrapping guaze.]* Cut off what you need. I'll look for the alcohol ... or perhaps some Neosporin Ointment!

EPIHODOV: Whatever you think best, dear friend.
      [LOPAHIN rummages through his shelves. EPIHODOV measures out a length of wrapping gauze and picks up an axe to cut it. GAEV begins to fondle the bookcase.]

LOPAHIN: Hydrogen peroxide? I seem to be out of alcohol. You cleaned me out last week.
      [EPIHODOV raises the axe and cuts off his hand.]

EPIHODOV: There! You see! I've cut off my hand! It's really quite remarkable! One thing after another!
      [FIRS mumbles something and sweeps up EPIHODOV'S hand. He begins wiping up the blood.]

LOPAHIN: Thank you, Firs.
      [LOPAHIN pours hydrogen peroxide on EPIHODOV'S hand.]

EPIHODOV: Ooh! It bubbles!

GAEV: *[To the bookshelf.]* Now listen carefully. Don't be alarmed, but... *[GAEV lifts his shirt to reveal a small pistol.]* I won't use it unless I have to, so ... remain calm. If you act suspicious, they'll know something's up, and then we'll have to come out shooting! Take a deep breath. Deep breath. Deep breath! You're going to give us away!

LOPAHIN: What's going on over there?

GAEV: Stay back! Stay back or I'll shoot! *[GAEV points the gun at LOPAHIN and EPIHODOV. FIRS begins dusting the bookcase.]* I'll use this if I have to! Now...we're going to walk out of here nice and easy. Nice and easy, understand!
      [GAEV lifts the bookcase and moves towards the door. FIRS dusts it as they go, mumbling to himself. As he reaches the

door, GAEV slips, and the gun goes off—shooting
EPIHODOV several times in the chest.]

EPIHODOV: You see! Didn't I tell you?! One thing after another!
But I don't complain. I'm used to it!
[EPIHODOV falls to the ground, dead—blood spurting from
his chest. GAEV shields the bookcase from this bloody
scene.]

GAEV: Don't look! Please! You don't want to see ... Oh, don't be
angry with me. I couldn't stand it if you were angry with me. They
drove me to it! Try to understand!

LOPAHIN: You killed him.

GAEV: Yes! I didn't mean to, but I must save this dear bookcase! It
has been with me since I was a small child! It is my only true friend!
Isn't that right, dear bookcase.

LOPAHIN: Oh, dear Leonid Andreyevitch. What a tragedy! This
particular bookcase is not your bookcase at all! Why, I know the
bookcase you speak of—it was sold to a traveling salesman the same
week your dear boring sister left us!

GAEV: No!

LOPAHIN: Yes. *[Pause.]*

GAEV: Then ... this isn't my bookcase?

LOPAHIN: Not at all. I purchased this bookcase from three sisters
who claimed to be moving to Moscow ... although I don't think they
were really moving anywhere. They talked of nothing else, but it
seemed a lot of empty gibberish to me.

GAEV: *[To the bookcase.]* You fraud! You led me on! You're not
my bookcase! *[He blasts the bookcase to pieces.]* I believe a man
should always be prepared to kill himself. That's why I carry a gun.

[GAEV shoots himself in the head.]

LOPAHIN: What a bloody circus. *[Pause. FIRS begins to clean up the mess.]* I remember when I was fifteen, the circus came to town. I wanted to see the circus, but my father thought it frivolous. I remember quite vividly. He took the whole circus and shoved it up my ass. Right up my ass!
> *[FIRS continues to clean, mumbling to himself incoherently, as the lights fade to black.]*

* * *

CPSIA information can be obtained at www.ICGtesting.com
Printed in the USA
BVOW021402180712

295531BV00003B/349/P